I0623119

The Divine Tragedy

Chai Mahfood

En Route Books & Media, LLC
Saint Louis, MO

En Route Books and Media, LLC

5705 Rhodes Avenue

St. Louis, MO 63109

Contact us at **contact@enroutebooksandmedia.com**

Cover Credit: Chai Mahfood

ISBN-13: 979-8-88870-150-8

Library of Congress Control Number: 2024935303

This book is dedicated to my Dad and Mom, my brother Xander, and my Nana for teaching me to write with intent to disturb the comfortable and comfort the disturbed (and my friends, the rascals that helped me design Jackson's personality).

Jackson had entered knowing what waited for him, and yet he persevered. He knew his purpose here. He did. And his purpose was to die. He would be a sacrificial lamb for the greater good. And he was okay with that. For the purpose was good. For he was good.

The cult's heretical voices played games with his mind, but he would not falter. Armed with a spiked bat and a rosary blessed by Father Ward, he would walk into hell's embrace and leave unscathed on the other side.

He awoke in a dark corridor. He couldn't see, but feeling his forehead he felt something familiarly wet and sticky. Putting it to his lips, he tasted iron.

Memories danced across his mind in elegant, graceful swirls. He could not recall his recollections ever being so clear and vivid as they were now. Memories of youth he'd long been told to repress, for they were his weakest moments. His lowest points. The moments when his faith had been the most fragile.

— — — — — —

They had arrived early to the drive-in theater, him and his life-long friend, Oliver. They had the time to spare to go on a short walk up the mountain.

They had stopped to overlook their tiny town. The cliffside was just a stone's throw away from the parking lot, guarded by a handrail for safety and overlooking large swaths of the Appalachian wilderness. An orange sky highlighted by pink-bottomed clouds and the sun set over the distant tree line that formed the horizon. His mother had told him something terrible, and all Jackson had felt after that point was the most intense urge to get away. To run and run and run until he never saw anything again.

He leaned against the railing, looking over the edge and wondering aloud how far the fall to the bottom would be. Oliver took his hand.

————————

He couldn't suppress the tears that rolled down his face as his father dumped dirt over the hole. His best friend, his childhood companion, now one with the earth. He couldn't bear it.

"Don't be so sensitive now, boy," his father said. "We'll get ya a new one real soon."

But Jackson didn't want a new one; he wanted Skye. He wanted Skye to be back. No dog would ever fill that hole in his heart. No dog could replace Skye. That rascal that ate off his plate and slept in his bed and would lick his ear to wake him up.

When his dad had gone inside, he sat by the makeshift grave, hugging tightly the little clay mold he and his sister had made. He thought Skye would live forever.

"It was the Lord's will," his mother said as she stepped outside. As though that would comfort him. "God needed him more."

That didn't make sense to him. If God loved his creations so much, why would he let them die?

He bit his lip to avoid another round of tears.

———————

There were quiet whispers among the pews behind them. A new girl had moved into town recently. Her name was Sandy. Jackson thought Sandy was nice.

He found it difficult to focus on the minister. Gossip was frowned upon in the ministry, but Jackson's mom had told him it was okay to listen so long as you didn't participate.

His mother scowled as the kids behind her jabbed at every part of her. Her dark stringy hair, her shoes, her dress, her skin, her belly. Especially her belly. He heard them make gagging and vomiting noises until she got up and walked off.

Jackson went to go after her, but his mother pulled back. "Don't." She commanded.

"But mom, she's hurt. She needs help," he whispered. "They were gossiping about her mom—she needs help."

"Don't." She said again, holding his wrist tighter. "That girl ain't right. You stay away from her."

Jackson felt confused and heartbroken, but he slowly sat down. To disobey one's mother and father was a sin after all. But his mother was so devoted to the teachings of the Lord. Why wouldn't she let him go to her? Sandy could have been hurt! He wondered why God didn't protect her from the others.

————————

He was not going to be a sportsman, his father was sure of that. He always looked so disappointed when

Jackson couldn't hit the ball far enough in baseball, or got tackled to the ground in football, or missed the goal in soccer. Even now, his father seemed disappointed at how hard he was struggling to keep up with him on their hike into the mountains. Jackson was huffing and puffing, his legs hurt, and the sun was beating down on his back. Yet as his father turned a corner on the trail through the ravine he stopped and ushered the boy over. "Jack, come here! Quickly!"

Jackson rushed over as fast he could, not wanting to see his father's aggravated expression. He turned a corner and paused. "Whoa... what is it?"

"A fossil," his father replied. "Perfectly preserved at that." He raised his hand to let his son touch it. Jackson smiled in wonder as his hand ran over the bumps and edges.

He was awestruck. He'd never seen or heard of a fossil before. The grand shape of the skeleton bewildered and enthralled him. The bones of a mighty beast were right here, lying in the side of a mountain and perfectly exposed to them. He wondered if it was God's will to have them find it. "What kind of animal is it?" he asked.

"Well, some scientists say that millions of years ago, massive reptiles called dinosaurs roamed the

earth," his father explained. "They all died a long time ago, but there's still so much we can learn from their bones."

"Why would God kill them all?" Jackson asked.

"I don't know," his father responded. He knew that tone. He knew his father wanted to say something else but didn't want to explain. Jackson held his tongue.

Why would God kill these creatures if he loved them so much?

———————

Jackson had stumbled down, his heart filled with a sense of doom. He couldn't stop laughing as the pain of something dark entering him filled his senses. The room felt leathery, like skin. There was a shape. It felt vaguely humanoid. It, like the room, felt like warm, damp skin.

He couldn't stop laughing.

———————

"Isn't it gorgeous?" Sandy asked as they stepped onto the ice. Jackson looked up from where he'd been rubbing his mittened hands together and momentarily fell breathless. The winter cold had frozen over the surface, painting it a foggy white and leaving it smooth and thick. Across its surface, the small waterfall that fed it was frozen as well, the running water looking like glass with only thin streams of its liquid form dripping slowly over the hanging icicles suspending the seemingly endless movement in time. The bare, snow-dusted branches of trees hung low over the waterfall and framed it under a bright, cloudy sky.

Sandy tugged on his sleeve. "Cmon, I said I'd show ya how to skate!" She smiled brightly. "Oh—oh, yeah," he chuckled sheepishly.

It was a difficult learning curve. Jackson blamed it on the ice. He was about as graceful as a baby giraffe first learning to walk.

They sat together on the ground for a long time after.

He didn't understand why his mother didn't approve of Sandy. Maybe God would change her mind. She was nice, she was good.

Why couldn't his mom see that?

———————

Their forms were frightening. Gargantuan and vaguely humanoid, limbs stretched much too long, skin much too tight, bones and veins much too spindly. The creatures stood side by side, leaving gaps too narrow for him to pass through. Silent vigils formed unholy barriers that he could not pass by. They did not respond to his word nor his cross, and Jackson felt himself quickly growing agitated. It wasn't until he looked around to see them stretching all around him that he realized it.

Not a barrier. A wall. Many walls. Trapping him within their unmoving perimeter.

Jackson clutched his bat tighter in his hand.

———————

"Leave it!" Jackson's mother tugged on his shirt harshly. The Appalachian mountains where something to get lost in, for anything. Bugs, animals.
People.

A little winter wren had fallen from its nest. It cheeped and chirped anxiously to get back to its mom. Jackson walked toward it, extending his arms. His mother pulled the back of his shirt harshly.

"What did I just tell you?"

"But mom-"

"Leave. It."

Jackson didn't quite understand. This bird needed their help. It had gotten lost. It needed to go to its nest! It was just a chick. Small and frail, like he was.

"It's God's will. It'll feed the dirt and soil, feed the worms and ants, too," she explained as she turned to go inside. The old wooden door closed behind her with a familiar creak.

He looked back at the little bird, helping it into its nest when his mom was gone.

God wouldn't abandon any of his creations.

Right?

———————

He had no way of knowing what had happened to the creature. It was perfectly still, wings splayed out on the ground around it, feathers ruffled. But otherwise, its body remained undisturbed. As though it had simply fallen out of the sky. Jackson's heart ached at the sight. His mother was never fond of pigeons. "Flying garbage-eating rats," she called them. But Jackson could not help but feel for them. They were but humble birds seeking any kind of way to get by. Hardly a being *worthy of such scorn or contempt. For they were one of God's creatures, loved and adored by him as much as any other. It deserved a proper burial. Like the cartoons showed.*

So, he went to the far side of his property and began to dig with bare hands. Tiny fingers pressed into the soil, tearing up clumps of grass and gathering the dirt in palms. Yet as he dug, he began to slow down, his mind racing with thought and concepts. If something as seemingly small and impertinent as a bird could die, did that mean people could die? Did that mean his family could die? Did that mean he could die? That he would die? Jackson's hand began to tremble.

He didn't want to die. He didn't even know what happened when you died! What happened when you died? Where did you go? What happened to your body? He dug faster and faster. Maybe the bird wasn't dead. Maybe it was just sleeping very comfortably. He began to huff and pant, the tears splashing down his cheeks as his mind spiraled into a whirlwind of uncomfortable ideas. Would he have to watch his family die? His mother? His father? His friends? He didn't want that. He didn't want to see them go in the ground—not unless they would spring back up out of the dirt like Bugs Bunny always did. Death wasn't permanent, was it? No, of course not! He wasn't going to die!

God loved him! God was merciful! God wouldn't let him die... would he?

Jackson shakily folded his little hands together, trying to pray between frightened sobs. For the bird, and for himself not to die.

He hadn't even started kindergarten, and he's already had his first brush with death.

———————

He thought he was going to be sick. The ride out was fun. He'd never been horseback riding before. But his father told them they weren't just here to ride horses. They were going to hunt.

The lot of him and his friends had found a fox and were going after it with their dogs and guns, shooting at the poor creature as it screamed and scampered across the hills, fighting for its life. The horses caught up to it so quickly, huffing and panting and whinnying as the men tried to guide their hooves over the frantic creature. In the end, it was not the horses nor the guns *that killed it, but the dogs. One grabbed the vulpes by its neck and brutally shook it in its jaws until the squirming and the screaming stopped. When it finally dropped the creature with a crack of one of the men's canes to its side, its head was gone.*

They all swore, furious that the dog had wasted "perfectly good meat" like that. Jackson couldn't stomach the sight. The fact that the poor creature had run so far, so fast, so desperately, only to be killed in such a savage, merciless manner made him gag. He slid off the horse, rushing into the bushes to hurl. Tears pricked at his eyes, a gush of bile and half-digested lunch fertilizing the ground as he fell to his knees trembling. His father groaned as he came over to pat the boy on the back, mumbling how he'd make a terrible hunter. Jackson made the mistake of looking over and was promptly sick again.

Clearly, the dogs didn't seem to mind. Two waited their turn as the first went back to roughly tearing the meat from its neck, enthusiastically devouring the stringy, warm remains of the creature it had caught.

Why God allowed such cruelty on earth he'd never understand.

———————

The prognosis had always been grim from the very beginning. The fact that this had been an inevitability, an expected event even, made the car ride back home from the hospital even more uncomfortably silent, just his mother and him watching the trees go by, their sad, dropping boughs hanging trembling in the autumn breeze as though sympathizing with the young man. He rested his head against the cool glass of the passenger-side window, staring glumly out into the blurring woods. The seatbelt was cutting uncomfortably into the flesh of his neck and doing nothing to stave the tears that wanted to well up on his lashes.

"It's not fair," he growled through grit teeth, frustration bleeding from his gums and poisoning his words with a sharp venom. Contempt for his situation. "Dad was fine yesterday."

"That's how it goes, Jack," his mother replied evenly. "That's how this disease works. One day, you're talking to him and helping him with yard work and everything's fine. The next, he's forgetting things. He's doing the same tasks over and over again. He

doesn't know who you are or where he is, and eventually, he hurts himself somehow. He's not your father anymore—"

"Don't say that!" Jackson suddenly raised his voice, ready to mount an aggressive defense only to shirk back at the sharp look his mother gave him. In an instant, she cut down his confidence, his determination. All of it—dashed with a single, wordless look.

"He's confused." She corrected herself, turning her attention back to the road. "And he's only going to get worse. Just like his mother. And his grandmother. They all turned out like this."

Jackson suddenly felt faint. "Does... Does that mean it's going to happen to me, too?"

"Probably." His mother responded, not a note of hesitation or concern in her voice. "You have a long time before that happens. Better that you know the signs now though anyway."

The car was quiet for another long spell. Jackson stared over the dash at the road ahead, as though trying to see forward in time to when he became like his father now. Shambling, mumbling, straining to lift minor things without his arms shaking. Heading toward the stairs without his glasses on and missing that first fateful step at the top. Would he have a son of his own to yell his name and reach for him, only to fall short and watch in horror as he tumbled down the stairs? Would he remain frozen in time, watching him groan and writhe in agony, before finally screaming for his mother? Would Jackson have a wife to gather him up—calmly and quickly—place him in the car, and drive him to the hospital for treatment? Would he survive the trek? Would he be okay? Would his family?

Would his father?

"Is dad ever going to come home?" He asked, looking down at his palms.

"Of course," his mother said flatly. "But he won't get better."

Jackson didn't want to believe that. He wanted to pray for the Lord to help his father, to make him better. To make them a family again like they had been years and years ago.

But somehow, he knew that wasn't going to work.

————————

Gluttony had been the one sin Jackson could never understand. All the others seemed reasonable. One could give into their wrath and pursue violence as a

means to get what they wanted. Envy could drive peo-
ple to do terrible, vile things against another in the
name of spite. One could be so slothful that they ne-
glected their duties and caused the demise of others for
that lack of action. Pride was often the defeating factor
in so many ancient stories, with one's ego making
them believe they were invincible when they were still
only mortal. Lust was an obvious one—the uncon-
trolled carnal desires of one's baser instincts could of-
ten turn their lack of self-control into some truly un-
forgivable act of cruelty. Greed was a common sin that
he witnessed; refusing to help one's neighbor by hoard-
ing resources or kindness had left many a man,
woman, and child to die on the cold, unguarded
streets. All of those he understood. But he could never
seem to understand gluttony.

"Maybe it's because you hear it and think of food?"
Sandy asked, rocking back and forth on the swing be-
side his.

"I guess so." Jackson responded. "It seems strange
to think that you could eat so much that it hurts other
people. How can eating too much food be bad for oth-
ers? It's worse for yourself than anything. And it's not

like you can keep eating forever. You'd have to throw it all up at some point, right?"

"Yeah, I guess." Sandy looked down at her legs, rocking them back and forth to gain some momentum. Jackson didn't seem to notice her response to the idea.

"It sounds like an easy sin to avoid, though. As long as we don't eat too much, we won't end up like that fat guy on the bed in the picture. Right, Sandy?" He nudged her arm with his elbow, beaming at her. She finally looked up, offering a weak grin in response.

"Right."

The rest of their time on the swings was spent in silence. Change was in the air.

Jackson wondered why God made food a sin.

———————

The first time he'd been struck he was 7, spilling Kool Aid on the carpet and leaving the fabric with a permanent red stain. His father called him over calmly, his little feet tiptoed to him, standing in front of him patiently.

His dad had taken a paddle, and swung at his behind harshly, leaving red marks and bruises on the tender flesh. He then told him to clean up his mess.

The second time he was nine. His parents had gotten into an argument. It got too loud, and he snuck out of his sister's embrace to come to his mother's defense.

He remembered the impact of his father's open palm meeting his cheek.

The third time he was fourteen. He'd dropped a plate and the crash woke his dad from his nap.

He couldn't go to school until the swelling went down.

————————

As much as he hated to admit it, the day his father died was the biggest relief of his life.

They wanted to exhume the body. Jackson was dreading that moment truthfully. The moment when they pulled the wooden casket up and cracked it open to reveal whatever remained of his father within.

The funeral had been hard enough, witnessing his father's withered body laid to rest in a bed of flowers. He was used to people looking at peace in their caskets. But not his father. The man looked just as frail and weathered, agonized and exhausted in death as he had in life. His clothes did not fit him. His fingers were bony and thin. He'd lost so much mass from refusing to eat. His final days were spent quiet and catatonic in his recliner, staring blankly at the television screen and watching programs he hated. Though Jackson was certain he was beyond awareness of what it was at that point.

He had fought so hard to be himself. The house was still littered with sticky notes he'd made for himself explaining basic tasks—locking the doors, flushing the toilet, washing his hands, putting on his glasses. His father had grappled with that demon of an illness, trying to force it from his mind as best he could. And yet, it seemed every time he managed to banish it for just a little while, the beast took some part of his mind with it. Those warm periods of lucidity where he could sit with his old man and talk just the same way they used to before became shorter and shorter. His mind grew less sharp, his hands grew less steady, his responses less and less clear until he could no longer feed himself, or walk, or even stand. The day he stopped responding at all was the day he knew the demon had won. The only call he would answer to then was that of the angels sent to send him off. And Jackson was blessed that at least he got to hold his hand as he went.

The funeral had offered him no closure. He cried then, and he still woke up crying even now. His dreams were haunted by the foggy, warm memories of his father and him. Their times spent together were the flickering flames of a cozy fireplace in his mind, warming his broken heart and his bleeding soul, only to extinguish when he awoke to remember that that fire would never exist again. Not truly. He had only the memory of its comforting warmth. There were no arms to run into when he was scared, no high-fives when he did a good job, no hand on his shoulder to squeeze and comfort him. His father was gone. And he wasn't coming back. And Jackson would cry over the ashes of that lost flame.

He didn't want to see the exhumation, but his mother wouldn't come alone. When they pried the casket lid off, nothing remained but the old bones of his father. Bits of flesh and hair still stubbornly clung to the skeleton. The smell was God-awful, the wretched stench of decay wafting up so strongly it made his eyes water. And yet somewhere under it all, he could still smell the cologne he'd been spritzed with before he was buried. The only sign that it was still him.

It was a relief because he was no longer hurting. Despite the pain he'd caused Jackson, the boy was glad to know his father would no longer be in pain.

As if that made him feel any better.

Jackson fell to his knees sobbing, asking God why He had done this.

———————

He felt liquid on his cheek, filling his eyes with blurry darkness. He wished he was a kid again, cause even if it was hell it was good. And when it was good it was *Good.*

He stood up, feeling the wall for a crack, a break, anything. He stumbled over a deep crack in the floor, looking down he realized he could now see his feet.

I have to jump—only way out, c'mon Jack ya can do this. He thought, backing up and leaping down with a running start. The wind generated caused his hair to whip around painfully, hitting his face repeatedly with its split ends. He tried to scream, but all the wind got sucked out of his throat before he got the chance. He collided with the floor with a loud echoey thud that rang through his ears as he lay there open to attack at any moment, but he couldn't muster the strength to move.

When he could finally get up, and when the dizziness and ringing in his ears cleared out, he raised his head, feeling the warm liquid of blood trickling down various body parts and staining his clothes. The room he found himself in was more like a corridor, with long, old stone walls and darkness in the distance. He felt uneasy as he gulped. His eyes were already well-adjusted to the darkness, but he couldn't see *well*. It felt odd as he got up to start walking, his body aching in all the worst ways possible.

The hallways opened up into a grand room. Sweeping black marble floors gleamed from the red light overhead as well as the brightly-burning sconces mounted on walls, which were carved with ornate images of demons and their symbols. Jackson squirmed under the many gazes of the stone eyes chiseled within the walls, turning his attention instead to the large statue that occupied the center of it. It depicted some fiend, the hair of his beard twisted into a tightly coiled braid pulled back just enough to reveal a mouth full of sharpened teeth. Elf-like ears sat back, pressed firmly to its head like a snarling animal. Just above, a pair of wide-set horns spiraled up as if cursing the sky. Its muscular torso sat with two arms extended, around each wrist dangling a chain with a platform hanging from the thick links of steel. Jackson approached them, noting how each had a deep divot in the shape of a dish. He approached the frame of the demon and realized the set of intricate symbols, fractals of rhombi, carved into his abdomen were actually the markings of a door with yet another divot in its stone face—a map, of sorts, of what it contained on the other side of it, a map of doors within doors within doors. He peered down at an inscription marked in red.

DELIVER TWO INTO MOLOCH'S HANDS BEFORE OPENING HIS NAVEL

Two? Two what? He felt nauseous as his mind quickly jumped to guess at what it meant. Still, he pressed on searching the room for any sort of lost item that might be worth resting in the dishes. Alas, he turned up nothing. But he did find that there was another hallway that stretched further on behind the statue, and he wagered that whatever it was he was looking for, it was likely to be found somewhere further down that dark path. Jackson swallowed, steeled his nerves, and pressed on down the hall. His heart beat loudly in his chest. His ribcage felt like it would break with how fast his heart beat. His lungs felt like there was nothing in them, and he feared his stomach wouldn't keep his food in for much longer. But he had to go. There was no choice but to keep walking. Despite how much he wanted to leave, despite how much he wanted to run away.

He followed the ever-continuing path of rhombi into a T-shaped corridor. At its end, another statue he'd learned had been charitably donated by a Save Family. The obscured face of a nun, who was cradling the body of a vessel with an outstretched arm emerging from a hole in its face, threatened to leave Jackson hyperventilating, for it looked far too much like Sandy. He turned away from it, coming instead to rest his back against one of the columns that framed the small area. He focused on steadying his breathing and drew his cross from his jacket. Wide brown eyes studied its features, counting the grooves and dents in the copper surface to calm himself. Jackson had not felt such paranoia as this in a very long time. And yet, he could not stop here. For his journey was still far from over. After he was certain he would not faint and his breathing was back to an acceptable rate,

Jackson stood up and moved away from the pillar toward the Western hallway.

What was it about this place that filled him with such dread that he couldn't help but doubt himself? Doubt his faith even? He was a lone lamb among this field of evil, lost from his flock. But his Lord and shepherd would surely come to him and guide him back, wouldn't he? God had never left him astray before. He wanted to believe so anyway. But… all those memories, those old, sore feelings of abandonment, of betrayal, of hopelessness. They swirled so violently within the confines of his mind that it shook something in him. Something he couldn't explain. But it made his crucifix suddenly feel much heavier in his pocket.

Treading down the hall, Jackson passed a portrait of what looked to be a faceless nun sitting in a chair in front of a pair of opened red drapes. It was… an oddly mundane piece. Almost serene. Something that seemed like it would fit much more naturally in a museum gallery than on the wall of a cult's complex bunker. Still, something about the image unsettled him. He chalked it up to the lack of discernible facial features on the nun and opted to scurry along, offering it one last glance before stopping when he realized that something was... different now. The nun was no longer sitting. Instead, she was standing with her arms crossed. And she seemed closer to the camera than before. John shuddered and timidly looked away once more to ensure he was safe before stepping closer to the picture. He looked back and gasped. It was a completely different image now. Now, the nun was barely recognizable. Her body and her robes were bursting outward into a million vaguely limb-like shapes, which were taking form around her into something far more insidious, something UNSPEAKABLE. The realization startled Jackson into falling back. He scooted away from the image, momentarily losing sight of it. When he looked up, it was gone.

His heart pounded as he looked around. His throat tightened with intense cries that begged to come out. He just wanted to leave now, forget the mission, forget it all. He had half a mind to run and keep running until he ran out of road and had to start life over with a new name.

He looked up at the nun one more time. In its place hung a gory, mutilated face. Its eyes glowed a menacing red, and it peeled itself from the wall and lurched toward him. Jackson scooted further down the hall, legs kicking wildly in an attempt to stand up again. After several agonizingly long seconds of willing his body to coordinate with his mind, he managed to stand and raise his cross. But the demon persisted, coming closer and closer, until he was forced to run down the hall to create some distance between him and the face. Broken Latin words tumbled from his lips in a desperate, sonorous cry as he willed the demon to yield to the cross. It drew close, its rancid breath wafting over his face and his trembling hands before it finally seemed to relent and retreat into the blank wall. Jackson stayed there for a moment, stunned by the sight. He wanted to collapse, but somehow his legs kept him up. He couldn't keep collapsing. His knees were already sore and bruised as it was. And now was not the time to break down. Press on.

A broken T-shaped corridor lay beyond, branching both further West and North. He lingered on the Westward path, passing by a Baphomet statue with hollow eyes that yet still seemed to fixate on him like a hungry wolf fixating on a tender lamb in an unguarded flock. Jackson shuddered, keeping his head down as he passed it by with a meekness to his gait and entered the next room. He paused at the sight of the statue. A morbid serpent coiling someone in its tendrils. The presence surrounding it was nothing short of ominous; Jackson was just as quick to skirt past it as he had been with the Baphomet. The very last room held a set of stairs down to a lower level. On it, another offering to Moloch. Jackson was suspicious of how easy this appeared to be and tentatively started down the steps. Yet, as he raised the offering piece from the floor, nothing happened.

Not at first, anyway.

His breath ran ragged as he looked to his left and at a depiction of some skeletal beast carved into the wall. Its hollow eyes glowed red and a grim chuckle echoed through the room. Jackson began to dart his gaze around nervously, waiting for something to jump out of the dark corners and dive at him. But nothing came. And after several agonizing minutes of waiting with his treasure in one hand and his cross in the other, he started up the steps and back toward the room with the serpent. He passed it by without incident, yet as he walked into what should have been the hallways, he found himself back in… the same room. But this time, another accompanied the first. What looked to be a writhing, sickly cultist in a robe.

Somewhere faintly in his mind, he heard a voice whispering.

QUOD TU ESTIS. FUIMUS TALIA.

Jackson shook his head quickly and started through the room. Again, he passed without incident. And again he found himself back at the far end of the same room. And yet again, he found another statue had appeared, pushing the first aside. What looked to be a cultist shedding their mortal head in favor of some warped, clawed appendage taking its place. The mere sight of it turned Jackson's stomach, and he quickly moved to the next room, praying that it would be the hallway once more. But it wasn't. Rather, it was a new room where he found what appeared to be a lone, dazed cultist. The acolyte seemed blind to him at first, completely unaware he was no longer alone. Jackson cautiously approached, hand gripping the crucifix in his pocket tightly.

No sooner had he stepped into their field of vision than they began to move and change shape, their jaw unhinging to an impossibly wide length, their eyes rolling back until all that remained were the strained, veiny whites. From their mouth escaped their organs, twisted and gnarled into a slimy, disgusting mockery of a large hand. Just like the statue. It launched out toward Jackson, and he narrowly avoided its grasp by jumping out of the way. Blinded, it groped around uselessly in search of his tender living meat, unaware of the cross raised against it until it was already sizzling and burning from the radiation of its holy influence. To dust it dissolved, leaving behind only smoke and an empty set of robes. Jackson was stunned, but this time, he could not even bring himself to spare an extra moment to pray for the individual. He simply pressed on in hopes that walking would stop his legs from shaking. Back past the corridor with the Baphomet, Jackson stopped once again at the room with the Save statue and paused to rest himself once more.

He stared at the piece he had collected, turning it over in his hands. So much trouble for just one part of this sick puzzle. It was truly a paltry reward. A joke more than it was a symbol of progress. Jackson wondered how much deeper he would have to wander into this Hell before he got some answers. Before it was over. How much longer could his faith hold out? He felt it crumbling in his grasp, breaking apart in his hands like rock sugar. Slow but steady. Leaking from his weak heart all over the floor, the light within him slowly being caressed and swallowed by the seemingly infinite tendrils of darkness within this place. He wanted to cry at the thought. Some lamb of God he was.

He wanted nothing more than to leave, but a dark apathy grew inside him, like he was accepting what was happening, more so, that he was accepting that this was a fight he would not win. He didn't seem scared of his death anymore, less scared, more unbothered, the thought of dying here seemed inevitable, unavoidable, and he wanted nothing more than to just give up and lay down, and wait, and wait. It would feel so good to just sit down and wait. It would feel good to die.

And yet, somehow, he found the strength to persist and push onward.

Passing through the Eastern hall, Jackson stopped to see another picture hanging on the wall. In the night sky, hung a full moon casting its bright, silvery glow down on a distant church on a prairie. In the foreground, what looked to be a nun on the path toward said house of God with her back turned to the camera. Just like the first, it seemed an odd choice for such a place as this, juxtaposed to the nefarious goal and infernal motifs of the organization which inhabited the labyrinth where it hung. And just like the first, when John chanced to glance away from it briefly, it, too, changed. The moon waned to a crescent shape and the nun turned to reveal carved and bloody features. Despite the previous experience, John still shuddered at the sight, swallowing nervously as he looked away and back once more. He found the moon eclipsed with a red halo about it and the nun standing closer again, her face mutilated to the degree where stringy, gory flesh hung about in stands across the gaping cavernous hole that was her face. When he looked away once more, he found relief in the fact that the painting had disappeared completely with no trace of the face left behind. And so, he pressed on eastward.

Another three-hall corridor, another Baphomet statue at its center, watching over the three paths at their intersecting point. This time, John was able to disregard the statue's piercing gaze and continued further eastward first. The first room he passed held another cultist who traded their face for a limb constructed of their innards. And just like the first, John dispatched of them quickly and without any hesitation. Further down the hall was a room where a demon sat in the far corner. Beside it, a sparkling eye that certainly belonged to Moloch. He stepped forward, pausing as he heard something crinkle under his foot. He leaned down to pick up the note, squinting as he read it.

**LET'S PLAY
RED LIGHT
GREEN LIGHT**

Jackson swallowed anxiously and looked back up at the creature in the corner. This game was never a strong suit of his. He was so poor at reading people and anticipating when and what they'd say. Still, he supposed he had no choice in the matter and nodded slightly at the being.

"Green light."

Jackson cautiously stepped down the stairs, clutching tightly the rosary around his neck. His feet shuffled anxiously, his anxiety rising with every small step he was forced to take toward the being in the corner. His palms were sweating, his legs were beginning to shake, and his breathing was growing uneasy.

"Red light."

He froze, stiffening up immediately and holding his breath as the being turned around. The cloak it wore obscured its face, yet somehow he could still feel its gaze boring into him. Studying him for the smallest twitch or falter in his gait. No doubt so that it could pounce on him and tear him to shreds with whatever twisted claws it hid under its robe.

"Green light."

It chimed, turning back around. Jackson took a second to breathe and hesitated before finally moving forward. The mask was so close. He was already halfway across the room. Just another step or two, and he'd be able to reach it if he could just—

"Red light."

He froze again, suspended on one leg and positively mortified. His sense of balance was terrible and yet, somehow, he was managing to avoid swaying. But he didn't know how long he could hold still. Every second felt like an eternity. Clenched muscles screamed for him to move and settle into a more comfortable position while his frantic mind reminded him that if he moved, he was dead. His breaths were shallow and shuddered. He struggled not to whimper as sweat streaked down his face. He couldn't hold this position any longer, his muscles twitched under his clothes and failed him, and he could not fight the sob rising in his throat.

"Green light."

That sob escaped him and Jackson stomped forward and swiped the piece from beside the demon, quickly shirking away from the burning heat of its presence and turning to move back to the stairs. He had won.

"Red light."

He stopped dead. It wasn't over?! Why, God? Why? Why him? Why did he have to suffer this way? What had he done to be trapped in this Hell? Behind him, he could feel the presence of something greater creeping up, but he couldn't move. He couldn't turn around. The tremors began and Jackson found himself sweating even worse than before. The darkness of the presence made his very soul itch and tingle with him, adrenaline pumping in his veins telling him to run. **Run. RUN!**

"Green light."

Jackson dared a glance over his shoulder and promptly felt the color drain from his face. That shape. That gait. The horns, the fangs peeking from hard gums, the burning eyes. It was Alu. Just inches away from him. A burst of terror overcame him, and he bolted like a scared deer, just escaping the reach of a clawed hand that swiped to grab him.

"Red light."

The words went unheard as Jackson ran. But he certainly heard the furious screeching of the other demon as it rushed after him, hissing and snapping with unseen jaws, quickly gaining ground and even surpassing the other shambling goat demon that pursued him with such deliberate slowness. Jackson rushed up the stairs, nearly tripping, but did not stop. He charged back through the corridors in a wild panic like an animal being pursued by an unrelenting hunter. He ran so far and so fast that he didn't even think to mind the two cultists that now lingered in the room where he'd exorcized the previous one.

Only when Jackson reached the T-shaped corridor with the Baphomet did he stop, doubling over with hands on his knees and panting. When he looked back, he found he was alone. He lingered, waiting for either demon to appear, but they did not come. Straightening himself up as best he could, he let out a long sigh. Lord, this was becoming too much for him.

He waited a good while for his hands to stop trembling and headed north, following the silent path of the corridor until he reached a new room. This was a room of cages surrounding yet another odd statue of a cloaked figure bearing the same eye as the Unspeakable with two hourglasses on its shoulders. In the flickering light of the sconces, he could make out the shadowy shapes of cultists hunched over behind the cold iron bars. Jackson whispered to them, trying to get their attention, but no matter what he said or did they did not cease their hushed murmuring. He stepped back from one cage to try the other, to no avail. They were lost, and they did not seem to wish to be found. He was mortified and yet saddened. And still, some part of him was angry. He scoffed. "If Gary loved you so much, then why are you in a cage?"

Yet he found himself asking himself that, too. If God loved him so much then why was he here? In this cage?

A dark chuckle echoed through the room, and Jackson felt his blood run cold with terror. He turned and out from behind the statue stepped yet another robed figure. But this one was... different. His face was obscured, but Jackson could still make out his wide, glistening grin and the simple eye symbol marked into his hood in the low light. He carried a pitchfork and yet, rather than use it as a weapon, he walked with it like a cane. This was not just any cultist. He was someone more important. And more dangerous if how casually he walked about the room was anything to go by.

"They're new initiates." He said casually, turning his back to the young man and stepping over to the cage on the far end of the room from Jackson to study the crumpled follower within." **Indoctrinates who were... hesitant about joining, shall we say. They needed a little extra help and guidance learning how we do things."**

He seemed to sense Jackson's horror without even needing to turn and spy on his expression. **"Oh, don't worry. They have people tending to them. The same people that brought them here in fact. Soon, they'll be ready. And they will make such fine acolytes. And you-"**

The man perked up, still keeping his back to John." **You'll make a fine sacrifice."**

"You... You **monster!**" Jackson raised his cross at the other man. The other seemed to predict his movement, as before his arm was even fully extended, the cultist spun on his heel with his pitchfork withdrawn and swiped it at him. Jackson narrowly avoided the swing of the pointed blades by jumping back, and then out of the way as the other stabbed at him with it. He stepped back from the cages, trying to put as much distance between him and the cultist as possible. Out of range of his pitchfork at least. It did little to help when the other rushed at him. Jackson yelped as he sidestepped to avoid being tackled.

Still, he wasn't fast enough to avoid the back-swing of the other's weapon. Cold iron bit into his side and jerked his whole body back with bruising force. Jackson hissed, gripping at his side with a silent prayer that none of his ribs were broken. He stumbled against the back wall of the room, holding it for support. As he looked up, he flung himself aside just in time to dodge another attempted stab with the pitchfork. He was sure it would have gutted him if the way it so easily sank into the stone wall behind him was any indication. He heard the man curse under his breath as he moved closer to pull his thrown weapon out of the wall. And Jackson was frightened by just how easily he managed it.

Frightened... but also **fascinated**. Mesmerized even. There was something about the strength the man must have possessed to be able to wield such a heavy, detrimental weapon. Jackson couldn't help but marvel at the thought.

But he was scared. So scared he felt tears roll down his face as he dodged and avoided the attacks. And as he saw the man turn toward him, he snapped from his momentary daze. He gasped and moved across the wall, leaning hard against it and spinning himself around the corner into another hallway. He

a second time and Jackson wailed in despair, terrified of the inevitable agonizing sensation of it biting him in half.

And yet... it never came.

When he finally dared to open his eyes, Jackson found himself startled by the fact that he was in one piece and was no longer falling. Rather, he was sitting. Sitting on the padded floor of a padded room. He tried to stand but found his arms could not be moved. When he looked down, he realized why. They were painfully compressed to his sides by a straitjacket.

A new kind of anxiety took hold of Jackson at the realization. Immediately, he began to squirm and struggle against the restraints. He was too afraid to call for help. On the wall behind him were countless crosses etched into the puffy surfaces. The padding was even torn away in some places, exposing the symbols that had been carved into the exposed concrete behind it. He struggled and strained to rise to his feet, jumping away from the wall. His gaze shot toward the door where he heard the squeaky wheels of a medicine cart and the muffled voices of doctors and nurses approaching behind it. The handle of the door jiggled and, without a thought, he bolted to the far side of the room. The wall suddenly shifted and dropped down, revealing a hidden hallway behind it. He raced down the unlit path, slamming into another at the end of it. He staggered back, dazed by the move, and turned the corner running again. A bright light suddenly overtook him, and he found himself collapsing onto the floor of his childhood home.

———————

"You clumsy boy," his mother stated weakly from her rocking chair. She looked so small and frail, huddled in her thick blanket with her cap pulled far down on her head. Despite her weakness, her tone was still sharp and cutting. "I pray you're light on your feet with wings."

Jackson rose and dusted himself off, realizing that his hands were no longer clamped to his sides by the straitjacket. A meek apology escaped. "I'm sorry. I tripped."

"You always trip," she snapped back, lighting another cigarette between her lips.

"Mother," Jackson hesitantly started. "The doctor said you shouldn't do that anymore. It'll make your illness worse."

"Jackson. Look at me," she said flatly, holding open her blanket to reveal the shriveled form beneath. Her once form fitting dress now hung from her frame like long, flowing drapes. Her hair was gone. Her skin wrinkled and sagged. "I'm already dying. The doctors refuse to save me. My life is in God's hands now."

Something about the way she rolled her eyes at the mention of God made Jackson feel conflicted. He flinched as she spoke again, much more crassly. Irritated. "Now, be a good son for once and go get me a lighter."

Jackson hesitated but relented with a quiet 'yes, mother' before going off to fulfill her wish.

She was gone the next day. A peaceful, dignified death in her sleep. Despite everyone saying he should be comforted and feel grateful that her passing was so kind and gentle, it did not stop Jackson from sobbing over her open casket. The stares he received, the disapproving looks sent his way as he cried over her lifeless body in a bed of flowers, did nothing to dissuade him. His aunt's hand on his shoulder insistently tugging at him and her mumbled words that he was 'making a scene' did not stop him.

Their judgment, for once, meant nothing to him. Only God could judge him after all. And he found it quite cruel of them that they would.

His mother was dead.

—————————

Had Jackson asked him, he would have done anything for him. John would have moved mountains, leveled forests, tamed the sea, and caught the moon for him. Jackson was his dearest friend. His most trusted companion. His first love for whom the flame had never truly died, no matter how hard he'd tried to smother it. So, when he sent for him, speaking of cult-like neighbors and paranormal happenings in his new apartment, he dropped everything to be with him. To help him.

To protect him.

He'd been expecting something truly horrifying. But this... this just broke his heart.

The sight of Jackson screaming, hunched over with contorted, clawed limbs. His teeth were sharpened to unnaturally fine points, his eyes overtaken by a deep red and dripping blood, his cheeks torn unnaturally wide. His normally beautifully kept deep brown hair was messy and unkempt—the nest for two gore-red horns, gnarled and twisting out of his skull. His back seeped blood as two bony wings, dangling with stray viscera, sprouted and flapped uselessly from his mutilated shoulder blades. He shambled on uneven legs toward him, retching and howling with the voice of the demon within him.

Alu.

John held his cross up, garnering every last bit of his confidence to shout the words of the 91st psalm at the infernal beast occupying his innocent husk. The creature taunted him with laughter, ever-resistant toward his holy influence and ever-amused by his display of forced bravado. They danced their dance, the beast fleeing from him into a statue, and then into him. It sank its talons into the recesses of his mind, whispering wicked wishes and whims into his ear, forcing him close to Jackson and hissing awful commands to him.

Kill him. Do it. Eviscerate him. Maim him.

And all the while, he could barely hear his muffled voice through the howling.

"FIGHT IT, JOHN!"

At long last and with one final agonized scream, he forced the creature's hand from his soul and cast it out into the open, screaming holy Latin at it until it finally retreated with a howl that promised the young preacher had not seen the last of it. A moment of tense silence fell over the duo, both panting and frozen in dazed terror, still processing what had just happened.

Jackson stepped out first, returning with a pair of cigarettes and some water and moving to sit on the floor beside him. They said nothing at first, simply brushed hands as they both stared off into the distance in silent contemplation. Finally, his soft, hoarse but sweet voice broke the quiet. "Thanks, John. I knew I could count on you."

The priest nodded. Neither looked at the other as he continued.

"Look, John. A man named Gary Miller runs this place. I think he's trying to summon some sort of demon. And after what we just saw, I'm convinced that you're the only one who can stop him."

A beat of quiet passed. John squeezed his hand and their gazes finally met.

"Do you need a place to stay?" He asked softly. Jackson smiled that same kind smile he always did and shook his head.

"I'll be fine. Go. Just… promise me one thing." His soft plea drew John to lean closer, his own gaze melting a fraction as he nodded again.

"Anything."

Jackson gently touched his cheek with the backs of his fingers.

"Please come back to me. Preferably still alive and in one piece."

They both shared a small laugh as their foreheads touched.

He found himself standing in darkness again. The jacket was tight around his arms once more and Jackson squirmed. As he looked around, he spotted a faint white light. Seeing nowhere else to go, he walked toward it. He didn't realize he was crying at first. The tears began to fall off his lashes, dripping down his cheeks slowly at first, then in a seemingly endless river. Jackson had to stop for a moment, attempting to catch its breath. But instead, all he could do was cry. And, so, he did. He began to cry openly and freely, his whimpers, his sobs, his inhales and wailing exhales echoing into the void all around him as he slowly sank to his knees and bowed his head until his forehead met the cold ground. Everything hurt. His mind. His head. His heart. His soul felt weighed down by so many burdens. There was so much he had tried to do, yet he always seemed to fall short. He had wronged so many with his own cowardice, with his lack of action, with his own inept shortcomings. It had cost him so many people so important to him.

His dog. His father. His mother. Eliza. Penelope. Sandy. Oliver.

Some good man he was, indeed. Too cowardly to be righteous, too indecisive to be reliable. How could he possibly have thought he could do this on his own? He was all alone down here in the darkest depth of the earth, practically standing at the edge of Hell's wide-open maw. Defenseless, weak, helpless, and hopeless. Faith had carried him this far, and with every step, he felt it dwindling. A leash—or perhaps a noose—was tied tightly around his neck, pulling him along by some overseeing entity that told him to keep going despite the bone-deep ache of his spirit's saying it could carry on no longer.

Even now, even in this sorry state, Jackson felt himself being pulled along by some otherworldly force toward the distant light. Tiredly, he rose to his feet, knowing that he could not resist it. He did not have the strength any longer. Yet, he persisted, sniffling and trying to blink away the tears that still blurred his vision until he was close enough to make out the sight of the pearly doorway. The pure white marble columns, the ornately carved symbols of cherubs blowing trumpets, and doves flying about. Jackson took it all in with blank eyes for a good long while, trying to feel for any warmth or comfort from it all. Any sign that this was truly a mercy sent from God.

He felt nothing. And some part of him was unsurprised.

Still, he closed his eyes as he passed through and let the light wash over him before fading.

When he opened them again, he found himself back at the room with Moloch. Seeing the familiar landmark of the demon statue, the red light and the dancing flames of the sconces, should have triggered another spike of anxiety in him as it reminded him once again of where he was. Yet, he could only feel a certain numbness as he regarded the model, moving from one hanging platform to the other, placing one of each of the three lost icons in the divots. He watched as one by one the chains ascended and carried the pieces up into his hands, where they ignited a roaring inferno. He lingered for a moment, watching the flames dance between his fingers. Briefly, he wondered what it might feel like to be consumed by that fire if for no other reason than to feel something or be rid of this horrid quest he'd been sent on. He shook the thought from his head, looking down to remember he still had one last piece. The key to his navel. Stepping forward, he slipped the shape snugly into its space in Moloch's abdomen and stepped back. The statue's eyes burned a furious red, its deep voice booming all around him.

MOLOCH IS PLEASED
WITH THINE SACRIFICE

The door sank in and rose with a distinctive sound like stone grinding against stone to reveal a darkened staircase leading further down into the labyrinth. Jackson peered into it with an uneasy gaze and felt a tingle run up his spine. In an instant, it felt as though all the emotions he thought he'd cried out into numbness came rushing back to him. The first among them to return?

Fear.

And still he pressed on, anxiously beginning to walk down the steps.

The darkness that stared back at him as he peered down the depths of the stairwell was unlike anything he'd seen before. Not even the eerie red glow of the labyrinth which seemed to permeate everything else thus far carried into the void which reached up from the depths to swallow the steps. Yet, despite the deep primordial fear the sight of it stoked in him, Jackson pressed onward and carefully followed them down. He jumped as the door slid closed behind him, the sound of grating stone making him cringe as he was left permanently suspended in the void. With no-where else to go, he made his descent with cautiously guided feet, feeling for each and every step as he went.

By the time he had reached the bottom, Jackson's eyes had finally adjusted to the low levels of light all around him. He was just barely able to make out the blank faces of walls linked together by sturdy chain link fences. He approached one to find only more darkness on the other side. With no gap at the top to try and climb over (Jackson wasn't sure he could even if there was—he'd not jumped a fence since he was a senior), he chose instead to rest his hand against the smooth surface of the wall closest to him and followed it to its edge before turning the corner. This lower level seemed somehow even more complex and labyrinthine than the maze he'd just been through on the floor above. And somehow even more unsettling.

Somehow, it felt even lonelier down here. Only the hollow echoing of his footfalls accompanied him. The reverberance here resonated even more than upstairs, his uncertain steps fading off into the darkness like bats flapping blindly into the night. For some strange reason he could not explain, Jackson hoped that he was not alone down here. For his mind could not comprehend nor cope with the thought that perhaps he was truly walking in isolation through these dark hallways. That holy presence of God he had been so accustomed to feeling on his shoulder before all this felt strangely absent. When or where it had flown from him, he did not know. But some part of him knew that it was gone now. That, on some level,

God had abandoned him. Sent him to meander these dark depths alone. Perhaps it was a test of his strength. Of his faith. But Jackson was weak in both body and spirit at this point. He yearned to feel some sort of comforting presence traveling with him. Something. Anything.

The thought should have made him panic. Perhaps it should have even disgusted him. But at this moment, the thought that perhaps even Gary might be down here with him brought an enigmatic feeling of relief to Jackson's chest. He would not know the man if he saw him, for he had never met him. And neither Lisa nor that creature in the basement of the clinic had described him in detail past his being "a normal human being." And, still, Jackson was so desperate for another presence to accompany him that he found himself genuinely comforted by the thought that even the vicious, brutalist leader of this cult might be down here with him. Watching him from the shadows. Poised and waiting for the perfect opportunity to strike. He wasn't sure what disturbed him more. The idea that he was being stalked like an unsuspecting prey animal…

Or that the idea didn't quite bother him as much as it probably should have.

He shook his head quickly and with a huff, trying to will the unexplainable heat from his face and press on without thinking too deeply about it.

Another turn down another corridor and Jackson saw a dim glow emanating from something somewhere down the hall. He looked back behind himself and felt his heart drop to his stomach. Somehow, this void-like maze felt even darker. As though all the light within it was being absorbed by whatever unholy influence was undoubtedly circling around it. Jackson rushed toward the source of the light, a hot wash of fear running over him at the realization of just how horribly frightful the infinite darkness was. As he came to a stop before it, he realized it was a lantern. An old, rusted metal thing with a worn glass casing holding the flickering flame within. The handle squealed as he pulled it up to hold out in front of him. Whatever relief the small light source might have brought him was dashed as he turned and caught a vague silhouette in the darkness. A shape that made all the blood in his body run cold.

Sandy?

Jackson gasped and stumbled back, the lantern swinging violently and the flame stuttering precariously at the sudden swing threatening to snuff it out.

When he looked back up, she was gone. A trick of the darkness on his unadjusted eyes. His breathing grew rapid and labored, and he dared to step forward again to search for her in the darkness. But there was nothing and no one there. And still, he realized he was more frightened by the prospect of there being no one there at all. Perhaps that was for the best though. After all, he was at a dead end. There was only one way to go from here and that was back the way he came.

And, so, Jackson started down that simple path, tracing back his steps and holding up the lantern every which way he could think of. The walls of this level were strangely blank. No carvings, no symbols, and no embellishments to the flat surface. Yet as he approached another intersecting corridor he'd come down from, he spotted something through the chain link fence. A figure that lingered even after several hard blinks.

He nervously approached it, trying to use the light to spy a better look at it, but to no avail. The intersecting shadows cast by the fence cut across their body, and anyways, they were too far away for Jackson to truly make out any of their features. He stepped back, feeling a cold dread creeping up his spine as he turned his back to the fence and pressed on. But then as he continued, he saw another. And another. And **another**. All sitting perfectly stock still behind the fence, all lingering just out of reach of the lantern's warm glow. It unsettled him, and yet somehow, he became accustomed to the sight. So much so that he found it strange when he finally saw a fence that wasn't occupied by a distant silhouette behind its links. That sight made Jackson far more anxious than any of the others. A trembling hand raised the lantern higher as he approached, breath shuddering as he peered beyond the gaps in the wires. It was quiet. All was still.

Suddenly, there came the loud cawing of a crow. It dove toward the fence from nowhere, a screech grating through the silence. Jackson threw himself back with a startled yell. The back of his head hit the wall behind him as he fell, and he cried out in pain, that aching throb from his last injury returning with a vengeance. He palmed lightly at the swelling, angry lump and looked up through spinning vision just in time to see it fluttering away, wings frantically beating as it vanished back into the darkness. He squeezed his eyes shut and opened them again, his

vision clearing just as one of those familiar silhou-
ettes emerged from in front of the fence. His blood
froze in his veins.

It looked like a girl—like Sandy. For a moment at
least. But it couldn't be. It couldn't even be human. It
bore a naked, skinny form. Its thin bruise-colored
flesh stretched over spindly bones that cracked when
it walked. It seemed nearly decapitated, head hanging
down over its chest with its face toward him, white
dead eyes on the sides of his head fixated on him as
it stumbled close. It let out a ghostly screech that
made all the hairs on Jackson's body stand on end.

He scrambled to his feet, disregarding the crack
in the glass of the lantern or how the flame within
fluttered and dimmed as he sharply turned and began running back toward the entrance. He swung
sharply around every corner, his footfalls hammering
all around him. The hallways seemed to spiral and
stretch on forever, yet the walls approached too soon,
and he always seemed to crash into them before
pushing himself off and stumbling down the next
path he found. He was, quite literally, running
blindly into the darkness. The creature hissed behind
him as he hit another wall so hard that it dazed him,
as though laughing at him.

The entrance... It was gone. All that remained was another hallway that most certainly had not been here before.

He fumbled for a moment to raise his cross at the monstrosity. His wrist trembled, and the words came out slurred and quick from his bleeding lips. It faltered for all of a second before pressing on toward him, and he felt himself truly weaken at the realization.

It wasn't working.

Why wasn't it working? Why couldn't he exorcize this one?

John sent him here for a reason—he said he'd meet him here.

Where is he?

More importantly.

Where is *he?*

It drew closer with another airy screech, and Jackson found himself stunned, knocked out from his train of thought. He spun on his heel and bolted down the hall, knowing not where it would take him or what would await him at its end. He only knew that he needed to run and get away from the fiend pursuing him. His blood rushed and his pulse pounded in his ears, deafening him to the sound of his feet hitting the pavement as it morphed into the crunching of leaves and dry grass underfoot. His lantern's light fizzled out and still, he did not think to slow down. Not until he saw yet more lights dancing in the far distance of his vision. He all but flew toward them, only stopping when he found himself engulfed in the warm light of a collection of large candles arranged in a halo around a large round seal on the ground.

Jackson finally stopped to catch his breath, his gaze darting back toward the way he'd come, anticipating the sight of that demon emerging from the shadows once more to torment him. But it never came. And Jackson felt grateful to whatever little influence of God still lingered with him for it to be. As he looked around, four paths highlighted by vigils branched off into the dark woods. Jackson paused to inspect them. Looks like he found a clear path for a change. He sighed and paused to open the cracked case of his lantern, using one of the larger candles to reignite the one inside. He waited until it was burning brightly once more before he finally stood up and held it out again to light his way.

To the East again he went, candlelight his only guide on this cloudy, moonless night. The silhouette of trees and their bare branches swaying in the wind proved difficult to ignore. Yet as he turned his gaze down, he found a reliable guide in the symbols scattered about the grass. They seemed almost reflective in quality, nearly glowing in the dim light. Jackson followed them until they tapered off into little more than bare soil with dried roots poking out. As he looked up, he found himself before a mutilated husk of a corpse seemingly suspended in time. Frozen. Motionless. He raised his cross on instinct and the figure seemed to twitch and writhe for a moment before falling from where it had hung in the air and crumbling to dust in the soil. Somewhere in the distance came an echoed thud. It sounded like it came from the seal. Jackson turned to return to the site and investigate it when that hellish figure emerged once more. Its hollow screech was joined by a cacophony of others just like it emerging from the darkness.

Jackson felt a burst of adrenaline explode in his vessels and jerkily jumped aside, avoiding a series of swipes from clawed hands. All too quickly, he broke and lost sight of the path, tearing off into the woods. The lantern rattled and creaked in his hold, its flickering light illuminating yet more of the figures meeting from the foggy tree line all around him. They chased him at a slow, steady pace. Ambling with such deliberate sluggishness, as if knowing that he would grow weak and tired eventually. Yet for now, he managed to somehow navigate the thick wood, finding himself before another levitating husk. Again, he raised his cross, and watched its muscles flutter before it fell to the earth in a cloud of dust and ash, releasing some silent key that broke part of the seal in the distance. And, again, a swarm of demons threatened to overtake him as he ran on and on through the dense forest. Somehow, he found a third shape. Another silent, still holder of an invisible force that loosened whatever grip it had on the seal as it crumbled at his feet just like the others. By now, the screeching was constant and ever-present, as ubiquitous as a violent night wind swirling all around him. Jackson felt nothing but the torrents of panic battering his body, threatening to overtake his head and drag him under their violent, inescapable waves. He didn't want to drown.

So, he ran.

He ran as fast as he could through the dead grass and the dry brush and the wispy branches of the forest, shoving them out of his way. He circled and weaved, realizing with horror that he was lost after just a short while. No matter where he turned, he could not find the paths of runes that had guided him into these woods. Their reflective edges were struck from his blurring vision. His only foreseeable salvation came in the faint shape of a building. A cabin? No—a shed! Without a moment spent for thought, Jackson flung the door open and slammed it shut behind him, shunting the handle of an old hoe in the slot between the arched handle and a low-hanging hook on the wall beside it. He stood back, watching through the cracked window and eyeing the door for any sign of the monsters beyond trying to batter their way in. Thankfully, after a moment of spotting and hearing nothing, he found himself able to breathe. He checked on his lantern, inspecting it briefly for any new signs of damage that might compromise its integrity and reliability. But there was nothing, and he heaved a sigh of relief at that fact. He raised it to look around.

The shed appeared to be an ordinary place. The walls were worn and weathered by time, and on them were hooks which held up a number of old tools. There were several workbenches tucked snugly up against the walls of the structure, and he came over to lean against one when he found a note. It was handwritten but seemingly never sent. A letter from Gary to some other. A message between allies in the dark arts. Part of Jackson cringed. Yet, he found another part of himself admiring the letter. More specifically, he marveled at the man's handwriting. It was neat and concise, the wording clear and the sentences written out in beautiful cursive. It seemed so strange to Jackson that a man of such evil could possess such strange beauty in the same stroke. No sooner had the thought crossed his mind than he was quickly dropping the note in an attempt to will away the thought. The only reason he found him admirable was truly because of the neatness in his handwriting, seeing as Jackson had never been good at penmanship. Other than that, he was irredeemable.

"You should be helping John now, not admiring the handwriting of a creep." Jackson chastised himself, frowning and moving toward the opposite workbench. Yet there, he found an even more interesting discovery.

A photograph. And not a very old one at that.

He set down the lantern on the chipped wood, using both hands to gingerly take the photo by its edges and raise it up to inspect it in the light. Three figures were caught in its frame. The one on the left was a man in a suit. His arms were tucked across his chest and his hair was swept back and neat. He would have seemed normal if it weren't for the rune carved into his forehead and the fact that his eyelids were peeled back. The one on the right was more mysterious. They donned a similar-looking coat paired with a scarf and a strange hat with a belt buckle on it. Their faces were obscured by a mask streaked with blood, their eyes barely visible through the holes. Yet, it was the figure in between and at the forefront of the image that held Jackson's attention. He was clearly a cultist. His deep red robes gave away that much. He was a well-groomed man, though—more than all the others he'd seen so far. His head was shaved and his goatee clean-cut. His eyes were hidden behind a pair of dark shades. Aviators? On his forehead was a rune in the shape of an eye. The top of one shape seemed to signify another was on his chest.

Jackson paused. Beyond the tingling feeling of confusion and fear he felt, they looked human but not quite. There was a sense of familiarity that came from looking over the picture. He felt as though he'd seen the man somewhere before, but he couldn't quite place where or when or how. Perhaps he was confusing him with another cultist. At some point, they all seemed to blend together in terms of looks. Jackson shook it off as a mere coincidence. A trick of his memory and nothing more. It was easy enough to dismiss as he set the picture down. It was harder to dismiss how he bore such resemblance to his father, causing his breath to quicken as his brain replayed every time his father—

Don't.

His mind wandered to John, his clerical collar and cassock, but when he wore his pajamas he saw a built figure in the priest, strength from his various exorcisms. It reminded him of how he felt when Sandy and he—

Dont.

"You shouldn't even dare to think about feeling for a man the way you do about Sandy. Much less a man like that. You despicable sinner…" Jackson scolded himself through grit teeth, He felt nothing but disgust and contempt now. More for himself than anything else. He picked up his lantern and angrily stomped away from the abandoned photo toward the door. He paused, anger momentarily quelled by the cautionary urge to check outside the window before stepping out again. As quietly as he could manage, Jackson pulled the makeshift lock from the shed handle and cracked the door open to peer outside using the light of the lantern to illuminate the world outside with just the thinnest sliver of light from the crack. Nothing. Not a trace of the monster. Jackson let out a breath he hadn't realized he'd been holding as he stepped out. A moment was spared to brush the dust from his pants, and he found himself back on the path of runes toward the site of the grand seal.

Or where it used to be at least. Now, all that remained was the halo of candles illuminating a circumference around a door. Jackson broke the circle and stepped forward to inspect it, only to be rendered breathless by the sight.

It was the very same door from his vision. Branded with the very same watchful eye and all. Its burning gaze gave him pause.

Did he really want to open this door?

Well, no. But seeing as he had nowhere else to go, did he really have a choice anymore?

"You're too far gone now." He joked wryly to himself under his breath. "Damned if you do, damned if you don't."

And so, he pressed onward and opened the door.

Stepping through the door felt as close to stepping through an impossible portal as anything else in this wretched place. Gone were the eerily still, moonless woods. Now instead, Jackson found himself surrounded by cultists. Their heads all bowed, their faces obscured by their hoods. They did not move. They did not speak. They simply stood, forming a sea of red on either side of him. And in the middle, a parting. A path for the Moses he had become to traverse in safety. Though that fact did little to take the edge off his nerves. Still, he knew better than to show weakness in the face of these devils, and he pushed forward. He passed row after row of still bodies, the flickering light of his flame bringing them in and out of focus from the darkness. He stopped only when he heard a familiar echoing voice ringing out around him.

"A riddle, young man: how do you make a portal to Hell?"

Jackson froze, breaking out in a cold sweat. The light of his lantern caught the shifting of flesh all around him. Bodies stood stock still, yet heads twisted in a series of writhing masses. It seemed as though the muscles and bone beneath the flesh of their faces were twisting and writhing restlessly, as though somehow trapped within the confines of their flesh, desperate to escape. The muffled squelching sounds that permeated the air all around him made him want to puke. Still, he persisted.

"Sometimes, it waits for the one who has already walked through it."

The lantern's light dimmed again suddenly, and Jackson gasped, anxiously tapping at the glass. It intensified again, thankfully. But to Jackson's horror, the sight it revealed was even more disturbing. Faces torn open, bodies began to writhe as fleshy tissue emerged in thick clumps of twisted viscera and muscle mass. They seemed to be trying to take shape, but the host providing them their mass simply did not have enough to offer to allow for it. The smell was unbearable. Rotting meat, decaying flesh, and some awful burning stench stung his nostrils and made his eyes water. And yet, still, he persisted. Somehow.

"Sometimes, it opens itself in the deepest, darkest room where nobody can find it."

The lantern's light flickered once more, nearly dying out completely before returning to reveal the most gruesome development yet. The bodies began to form chains of twisted organs and flesh. They mingled and writhed against one another. Malformed and veiny limbs clung to one another in a crude amalgamation of stretched meat. They twisted and knotted together, straining to merge and become some sort of fused superorganism, birthed from cruelty and darkness and chaos. The stench of it all was so vile, Jackson felt that he might faint. And yet, despite it all, he still persisted.

"And sometimes... it comes walking right up to you."

The lantern's light wavered one final time before snuffing out completely. Jackson felt the urge to sob climbing desperately up his throat. The urge to crumble and fall apart right then and there was nearly impossible to resist. Yet, something gave him the strength to overcome his despair. He peered into the darkness, and a set of shapes came into focus, so clear and so vivid, it almost dwarfed the lantern's dead light entirely.

The twins.

Jackson let out a shuddered breath and rushed toward the boys, hellbent on gathering them up in his arms. At long last, his quest was complete. His faith came fluttering back like a lost bird returning to its nest from a long migratory flight. And just when he thought it had come back to roost, the boys… disappeared. They vanished into the thick darkness like a cloud of dust. Jackson fell to his knees, arms still extended, lantern abandoned on the ground behind him and rolling away. He froze, panting, blood trailing from his cheek and his lip still. Whatever wings that small shred of faith had flown in on broke right before his eyes. And from beside him came a familiar dark chuckle.

Jackson raised his head, unsure of when he'd bowed it in grief. ~~Defeat?~~ He took a moment to blink and steady himself, before turning his head.

Had he not already been on his knees, he may well have fallen back from the shock.

"Hello, Jackson. It's nice to finally meet you."

It was **him**. The cultist from before. The one who had stabbed him with the needle, and the one who had nearly killed him in the room with the cages. And… And the one from the picture in the shed. Why was this one so insistent on following him? Surely, he wasn't of that much interest to one of Gary's lowly acolytes. Unless this wasn't just some acolyte. Unless it was-

No… It couldn't be…

"Lord, help me…" Jackson breathed out a desperate plea. "Somebody, please help me…"

He waited with bated breath, his eyes growing tearful as he began to tremble. He waited. And waited. And **waited**.

But no one answered.

Jackson watched Gary disappear as his body lay broken on the floor. Only a few hours ago, he was sure he would arrive at the other side of hell unscathed, for God protected all lambs of faith.

Now he wasn't so sure.

He wasn't like Dante. He didn't leave a survivor. He left a victim, a broken doll.

He was broken both physically and mentally, scared and shaking like a child. Jackson no longer desired to be a martyr, to be a sacrificial lamb.

He just wanted to get out.

About the Author

Chai Mahfood is a young St. Louis artist who has made a stunning literary debut with this novella, *The Divine Tragedy*.